Beware the
Evil Eye! →

and the
Evil Eyebro[w]

Very Bad Luck
to read other people's
diaries!!!

DON'T!

Daphne's Diary
of
Daily Disasters

by Marissa Moss

The
Name Game!

Simon & Schuster Books for Young Readers

New York   London   Toronto   Sydney

SIMON + SCHUSTER BOOKS FOR YOUNG READERS

An imprint of Simon + Schuster Children's Publishing Division

1230 Avenue of the Americas, New York, New York 10020

SIMON + SCHUSTER BOOKS FOR YOUNG READERS is a
trademark of Simon + Schuster, Inc.

For information about special discounts for bulk purchases,
please contact Simon + Schuster Special Sales
at 1-866-506-1949 or business@simonandschuster.com.

The Simon + Schuster Speakers Bureau can bring authors to
your live event. For more information or to book an event, contact the
Simon + Schuster Speakers Bureau at 1-866-248-3049 or
visit our website at www.simonspeakers.com.

Also available in a Simon + Schuster Books for Young Readers paperback edition

A Paula Wiseman Book

Book design by Daphne (with help from Tom Daly)

The text for this book is hand-lettered.

Manufactured in China

0411 SCP

2 4 6 8 10 9 7 5 3 1

CIP Data is available from the Library of Congress

ISBN 978-1-4424-2676-4 (hc)

ISBN 978-1-4424-1738-0 (pbk)

ISBN 978-1-4424-1965-0 (eBook)

This book is dedicated to
Paula Wiseman,
who started it all.

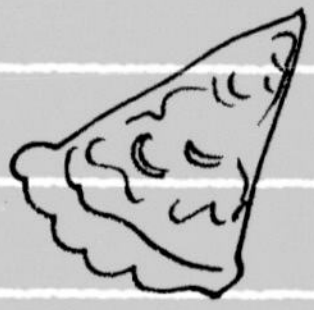

Yum, pizza!
The perfect food
for lunch, dinner, or
breakfast!

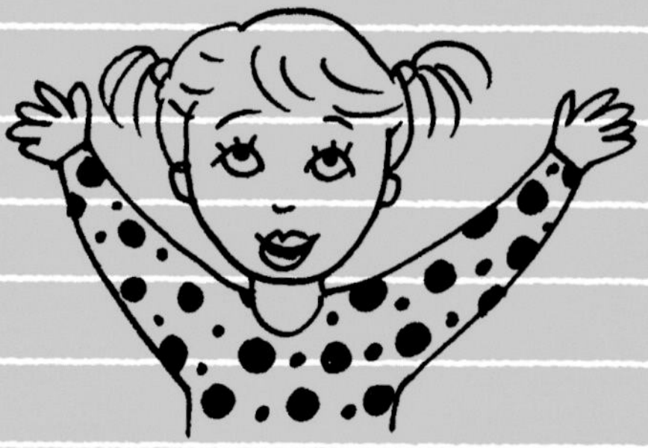

Name: _Daphne Davis_

Age: _9_

Grade: _4th_

Hometown: _Oakland_

Best Friend: _Kaylee_

Favorite Color: _Pink_

Hobbies: _Origami and collecting cute Japanese erasers_

Favorite Food: _Pizza (but NOT pepperoni!)_

Favorite Movie: _Back to the Future (or how to avoid any disaster!)_

Unfavorite Disasters—
the Worst of the Worst!

Daily Disaster, Thursday
1. Stepped in dog poop.
2. Tracked dog poop into school.
3. Went to bathroom and toilet paper stuck to dog poop stuck to shoe.
4. Trailed toilet paper, dog poop, and dog poop stink until recess when I could FINALLY scrape both off on the grass.
5. Have to keep on wearing these shoes because they're the only pair I have.
6. GROSS!!.

DAY ONE:

I wanted this to be my Diary of Daily Delights or my Diary of Days Worth Remembering, but my first day with this diary has been a total DISASTER! Just one bad thing after another, so that's what this is — my Diary of DOOM!

It could have been a diary of doodles, but it's not.

I could have added dairy to my diary, not disaster.

Who doodles cows anyway? Poodles for doodles maybe, but not cows!

I like doggy doodles!

It started out like this. It's my first day in 4th grade so Mom gave me this diary as a new 4th grader thing, along with the usual school supplies.

Diagram of a 4th grader
↓

Mom, Dad, twin brothers—there's room for all!

you can practically fit my family in there!

↑ enormous backpack for binders, folders, glue sticks, erasers, pens, pencils, hole punch, scissors, lunch—but can I still fit in textbooks?

I staggered to class, worried that if I leaned too much to one side, I'd keel over and never get up again without a tow truck.

I made it to my desk without crashing into anyone or anything—<u>not</u> easy, believe me! Then, just when I thought I was safe, disaster struck!

The teacher called roll.

Normally not something to worry about. Your name is called, you say "Here!", and that's that.

Except when it came to my name. Instead of saying Daphne, pronounced Daff-nee, like any civilized person with an average ability to read, she said. . .

"...Daffy?" DAFFY!! As in ditzy, dumb, dingbat—all kinds of "D" words that DON'T describe me.

I'm NOT a doughnut.

Or a dinosaur.

Or a doohickey— whatever that is.

And I'm DEFINITELY not a Daffy. I didn't want to say "Here" because that's not me. But everyone was staring at me as if it was really my name.

I stared straight ahead with a carefully b l a n k expression. →

Hmmm, who is that Daffy person, I wonder. Nothing to do with me, of course.

"Daffy? Daffy?" The teacher kept asking. Finally Zee pointed to me and said, "That's Daphne."

At least she said my name right. Which is more than I can say for the teacher who supposedly graduated from college and should know how to read.

I mean, it's only six letters.

But it was too late. The damage was done. For the rest of the day everyone called me Daffy. For the rest of my life, I bet.

I tried the old look-at-the-other-kid strategy.

It didn't work.

The only kid who didn't call me Daffy was my best friend, Kaylee.

She said the best way to get back at everyone was to give _them_ nicknames. So we did. It got pretty creative.

Sonna became
"Janitor"

Justin became
"Just-in-time"

Bob became
"Bobble"

Stephanie became
"Stuffy"

Vince became
"Blintz"

Carmela became
"Caramel Corn"

Lester became
"Pester"

Hannah became
"Hannah Banana"

Eric became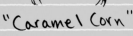
"Earache"

I admit most were pretty lame and none of them stuck.

After school, things only got worse. Mom took me to the orthodontist because I'm getting a pre-braces retainer. As if braces aren't bad enough! I think it's a racket for the orthodontist to make more money. Instead of simply suffering through braces, <u>first</u> I get to suffer through this stupid retainer. Then braces. Then a retainer again. I'll spend all my life at the orthodontist's!

Anyway, guess what name the dentist's helper called out when it was my turn.
Daphne? No such luck!
Daffy! Again! Twice in one horrible day!

I glared at Mom.

And that wasn't even the worst part!
Instead of the short woman with curly hair
and a big smile, I got the hippo lady.
   I call her that because she has no neck
and is really pink and looks just like a
hippo with
her blunt,
round nose.
Mom says
she's a cute
hippo, but
to me she's a hippo, plain and simple.
Which I guess would be okay except she
has thick sausage fingers that can barely
fit into my mouth. And her hair
smells like the kind of air freshener
you hang in a car.

I'm afraid
I'll choke!

While I was having my mouth stuffed with sausages, my brothers were tearing apart the waiting room.

Look at me! I'm a Jedi warrior!

Ha! You're a trash can warrior!

← David

Donald →

David and Donald are identical twins, both five years old and in kindergarten. There's only one way to tell them apart. The Booger Bubble. David always has a green bubble of snot hanging out of one nostril. Always. Mom says it's just allergies and he'll outgrow them.

I say it's just disgusting, but it's the only way we can tell David from Donald. We need that Booger Bubble!

Booger Bubble— gross!

Even though David and Donald are only five, they're already on a soccer team. They're obsessed with soccer. So where did we go after the orthodontist?

Soccer practice.

There is nothing more boring than watching someone else play soccer — especially when the someone elses are a bunch of little kids who can barely follow the rules.

sitting in the bleachers trying not to listen to the soccer moms' gossip

eyes glazed over in boredom

Mom says I shouldn't complain, just do my homework. That took all of seventeen minutes, leaving me forty-three minutes of watching grass grow.

↑ See for yourself how exciting that is.

So I decided to doodle instead. I was thinking of the hippo lady, so I started drawing the soccer moms like the animals they reminded me of.

↑
the horsey mom with the long face, big horse teeth, mane hair, and a voice like a whinny

↑
the snuffly mom with the pig nose, round cheeks, and squeal when she laughs — oink, oink, oink!

Mom saw what I was doing and told me
to stop it, it's not nice. I wasn't being insulting,
just creative. Anyway, then I had to think
of something else to doodle.

How about rebuses or picture puzzles?

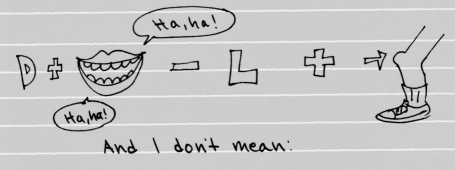

And I don't mean:

or:

My brothers yelled at me to stop doodling and watch how great they played soccer. And actually, they're not bad. They're even pretty good. Dad says they have natural talent. Unlike me. I'm terrible at every sport I've ever played and still I keep trying.

Except for soccer. I gave up on that after the time I was goalie and got hit by a ball in the stomach.

I did block the goal, but believe me, it wasn't worth it, and I'm not doing that again.

There was one good thing about soccer practice — the ice cream man.

Ring-a-ling-a-ling-a-ting-a-ling-ling

I love this ice cream man because he has flavors you never see anywhere else. Like Pistachio Bacon, Salt and Pepper, Beet Chocolate Chip, Horseradish Plum. Sometimes I try a strange one just because I'm curious, and you know what? It's always good. The Pistachio Bacon was a real surprise — but then, anything with bacon is delicious.

Donald and David always get the same old predictable thing. Vanilla (Donald) and chocolate (David). The ice cream man is wasted on them.

On the drive home, Mom finally asked the question I've been dreading ever since she picked me up from school.

"So, how was the first day of school?"

Lucky for me, the twins were so excited about starting kindergarten they babbled the whole way home about snack and nap time and reading circle and recess and sharing.

I wish I was back in kindergarten! Those days were so easy!

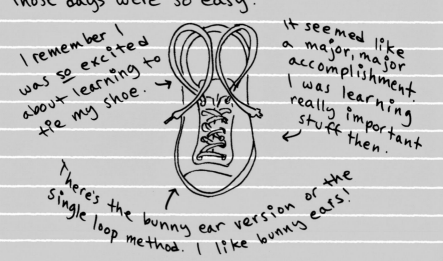

I remember I was so excited about learning to tie my shoe. →

It seemed like a major, major accomplishment. I was learning really important stuff then. ←

There's the bunny ear version or the single loop method. I like bunny ears!

"How about you, Daphne?" Mom asked after we got home.

"Well, we don't have snack or reading circle or any of that good stuff."

"You don't? Poor Daphne! She just has tests and homework," Donald said. Or maybe it was David. I wasn't looking to see which one it was, and their voices are as identical as everything else.

Sometimes I wonder what it's like to be them — like having a living mirror around all the time.

If one of them got called something dumb, like "Dopey," he'd just pretend to be the other twin.

"You know what I mean," Mom said. "Do you like your teacher? Are any of your friends in your class? Any enemies?"

Do I like my teacher? Is she my enemy? Apart from hating her for getting my name horribly, disastrously wrong, I'm not sure.

It's too soon to know. She might have the ingredients of a terrible teacher. Which are:

① Too much homework.
② Too many tests.
③ Boring way of speaking.
④ Impossible-to-understand strong accent.

Clazz, idz dime do stooding da zola zisteem!

I had a teacher like this once.
← She was exhausting to listen to.

⑤ Using way too many handouts.

C'mon, kids! Fill in the blanks and I'll fill in your brain — with more blanks!

No thinking necessary! →

⑥ Telling you about their personal lives in an embarrassing way.

I hope everyone had a relaxing weekend. I got food poisoning and spent all day and night on the toilet, emptying out one end or another. But I'm fine now, thanks for asking.

← We didn't!

⑦ Bad breath — bad in anyone, but with a teacher, it's a nightmare.

Trying not to breathe. →

Write neatly, please! I need to be able to read this.

Poison gas →

And I need to be able to breathe!

⑧ Too many PowerPoints.

That's a flower.

Flower

Leaf

That's a leaf.

Especially when the teacher just reads exactly what's on the PowerPoint without adding ANY new information. BOOOOORING!

As if I can't read it myself! Spare me the misery!

I hate PowerPoints — they're point-LESS!

⑨ and ⑩ Mean teachers — they count for double because they're the absolute WORST. They actually hate kids and become teachers just to torment us.

I have to admit my new teacher probably isn't like any of these — phew! But she's in her own category, the Can't-Ever-Get-Your-Name-Right one.

Anyway, I told Mom that yes, Kaylee is in my class.
"That's lucky," she said. "Now no matter what, it'll be a good school year."
No matter what? Even if I have to spend the year as Daffy instead of Daphne? Maybe even the rest of my life!

But Mom's right that even with a bad teacher, it's better to suffer with a friend than without. And if the teacher turns out to be good, it's still better to have a friend there.

Kaylee must have known we were talking about her because right then the phone rang and it was her.

Donald answered, the brother without the Booger Bubble.

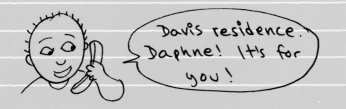

Davis residence. Daphne! It's for you!

I give Donald points for getting my name right.

"So," Kaylee asked, "what do you think of our teacher? I asked around and all the fifth graders who had her last year say she's nice. And not too much homework."

Kaylee

"Nice to them maybe," I said. "To the people whose names she can pronounce."

"C'mon! Are you still sore about the name thing? Believe me, no one will remember it by tomorrow."

"Are you kidding? It's the one thing they <u>will</u> remember! I'm gonna be Daffy forever now. Or until I move, go away to college, or something else drastic like that."

"You're exaggerating."

"If you're so sure, let's swap names. I'll be Kaylee and you be Daphne."

Kaylee laughed. "That's exactly what my sister said!"

Kaylee has a younger sister, not as young as my brothers, but still little. She just started second grade.

She has her quirks—like she only wears striped shirts and socks. I bet if they made striped pants she'd wear those, too. Maybe she wants to be a zebra or something.

"Did she have a bad first day of school?"
I asked. "Did kids make fun of her stripes?"

"Not yet," Kaylee said. "That usually takes
a few days. She had a problem like yours.
The teacher got her name wrong."

"Fiona? What could you say instead of
Fiona?" I ran through the possibilities in
my head. Mona? Fio-nay? Rhianna?
Leanna? Roxanna?

"Phony! The teacher called her Phony!
Now all the other kids are calling her Phony
Baloney Fioney. You can imagine how she
feels!"

I could. In fact I knew EXACTLY how she
felt. But I couldn't help saying, "I dunno.
That could give her a great idea for her
Halloween costume."

"Not funny!"
Kaylee said.

"I know. If only baloney
didn't have such a bad
reputation. Who's her
teacher? Maybe she can call
her Salami back — or Liverwurst!"

I'm lunch meat!

"Mr. Diggs. We had him in second grade, remember? He's a good teacher except for this. Fiona said he was super sorry he'd messed up her name, but it was too late. He couldn't unsay it."

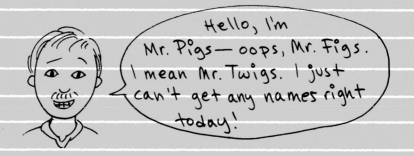

Hello, I'm Mr. Pigs— oops, Mr. Figs. I mean Mr. Twigs. I just can't get any names right today!

↑

He tried to make a joke out of it to get the kids to laugh at him instead of Fiona. Naturally, that didn't work.

I guess it's comforting to know that even good teachers make dumb mistakes. Maybe ours isn't so bad, even though she's ruined my life. That's what Kaylee thinks.

Then Dad came home and it was time for dinner and the same questions all over again.

How was your day? Do you like your teacher?
Are any friends in your class?. Blah, blah, blah.
I let Donald and David do all the answering.

Lucky hamster,
I thought. →

No one turns its
name into a joke.

Kindergarten is the best grade ever. You play
with your friends and have fun. No tests. No
homework. No mean teasing. Plus you get
hamsters.

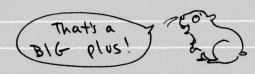

"What about you, Daphne?" Dad asked. "You're awful quiet."

"It's okay." I really didn't want to talk about it anymore. I wanted to forget it had happened. I hoped everyone else would, like Kaylee said.

So Dad started talking about his day, which is boring for everyone except Mom (and maybe even for her, too). Dad works in an office doing something, I'm not sure what, but whenever he talks about it, my eyes glaze over. I can actually feel my body fill up with boredom.

office stuff— all boring

stapler

files

paper clips— exciting!

At least Mom's work is something I can understand. She cuts hair in a salon. That's why we always have such good haircuts. And an endless supply of combs.

salon stuff— much more fun

scissors

gels and goos

combs

Dad was talking about some new guy in his office. Blah, blah, blah, BLAH! Then he said something that made me pay attention.

> So I introduced myself — you know, the usual. "Hello, I'm Dunston Davis."

> And he said, "Dunce?! Like a dodo? A dummy? A doofus?"

> "NO!" I said. "Like none of those! Dunston as in D-U-N-S-T-O-N."

"But you know," Dad said. "I have a funny feeling he's calling me Dunce behind my back. That's so fourth grade!"

"Exactly!" I yelled. Wow! I didn't know grown-ups got teased for their names, just like kids. But really, with a name like Dunston, can you blame the guy?

"What do you mean, 'Exactly'?" Dad asked.

"Well, I'm in fourth grade and that's EXACTLY what it's like. People make fun of your name any way they can."

"You've only been in fourth grade for one day," Mom said. "I'm sure it's different from third grade."

"Not that way," I said. "Names are always fair game for teasing."

"I had my time of name teasing," Dad said. "I think it's fair to expect that NOT to happen once you graduate from middle school."

Suddenly I thought of my dad as a → little kid with big glasses.

And a name like Dunston! He must have been <u>tortured</u> in school!

"Wow, Dad, I bet you really got it bad." I patted his hand to make him feel better.

"I don't want to talk about it," he said.

Ouch!

"Daddy's a dunce! Daddy's a dodo!"
Donald shrieked.

"Daddy's a doo-doo head! Daddy's a dummy!" David yelled.

"That's enough!" Dad stomped out.

"You boys go apologize to your father. Name-calling isn't nice — ever!" Mom ordered. She sounded mad but her mouth was trying hard not to smile.

The twins didn't notice. They thought → they were in BIG trouble.

They really did look sorry. But they were telling the wrong people.

I felt bad for Dad, still having to suffer from his name. After dinner I found him in his office, listening to music, looking like he was trying to forget even having a name. I know the feeling.

He was in his big recliner with a faraway look in his eyes. He calls this chair "Dreamland" because that's where he goes when he's in it.

"Hey," I said, pulling off his headphones. "What are you listening to?"
He pointed to a CD.
"Sublime?" I asked.
"It's pronounced Sue-bleem," he said.
"Oh," I said. "What a surpreeze."
I thought it was funny that I messed up someone's name. It's easy to do.

Dad laughed. "I guess my name isn't the only one that gets mangled!"

I laughed too. "Yeah, there's my name."

"Your name?" he asked.

So I told him what had happened at school today with my teacher and the roll call of Doom. Daffy.

So now that's my name for all of fourth grade, maybe even the rest of my life.

Unless we move.

"Maybe not," Dad said. "You have to give someone _else_ a better, funnier name."

"I tried. And anyway there's no one named Dunston in my class—too bad!" I teased.

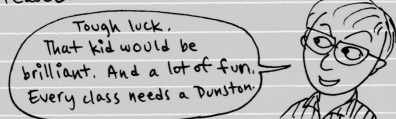

Tough luck. That kid would be brilliant. And a lot of fun. Every class needs a Dunston.

I told him how Kaylee and I had come up with nicknames for all the kids we could think of, but they were all lame, lamer, lamest.

Wait! I have a great idea!

One that will harm no kids and hurt nobody's feelings.

"What?" I asked. It sounded too good to be true.

"Don't make fun of the other students. You need to target the teacher!"

That sounded dangerous, NOT good at all.

"It's simple," Dad said. "You need a funny nickname for the teacher. Something that isn't mean or nasty, just absolutely hilarious. Believe me, teachers like joke-y type names. Now what's your teacher's name?"

I was still suspicious of the whole idea. It sounded like the perfect way to get detention.
  But I told him. "Ms. Underwood."
  "Oh, this is too easy!" Dad laughed.
  I tried to get what he meant. Underwood. Understood. Underworld.
  Then I got it! I knew why he was laughing. It WAS perfect!

UNDERWEAR!

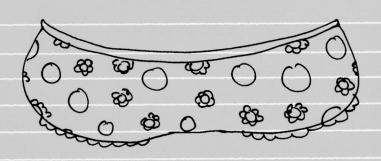

  Not only would EVERYONE call her Ms. Underwear, there was a playground song to go with the name. A joke and a song, all in one!

There goes Teacher floating down
   the Delaware,
Chewing on her underwear,
Couldn't find another pair.
Ten days later eaten by a polar
   bear,
That was the end of teeeaacher!

   I called up Kaylee right away and
sang it to her. She agreed it was
brilliant!

formerly Ms. Underwood

Now Ms. Underwear—
wearing underwear as
overwear on her head!

Now I'm actually excited to go to school tomorrow and put my amazing genius plan into action!

I had happy dreams that night all about funny names, and none of them were mine.

Cowla Cowsky

Wendy Weiner Dog

Missy Moose

Chicky
Buckbuckbuck

Then the names got mixed up with strange
ice cream flavors, like Pineapple Patty,
Chocolate Chip Charlene, Cucumber Ripple
Rodney, Butterscotch Biff, Licorice Lily.
   When I woke up, it took me a while but
then I remembered my plan. And that
put me in a great mood.

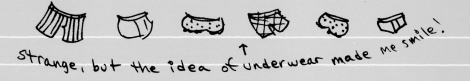

strange, but the idea of ↑ underwear made me smile!

I met Kaylee right before the bell rang.
"Are you ready?" I asked.
"Ready!" she answered. She was grinning as much as me. It was going to be a great day, I knew it.
Class started and before anybody could tease me about yesterday's nickname, I raised my hand.

Ms. Underwear...
I mean, oops...
Ms. Underwood,
could you please explain the class website again?

Ms. Underwood glared, but she couldn't exactly yell at me for something she had done herself. After all, it was an innocent mistake. Mistakes happen. She should know!

Then Kaylee raised her hand.

Ms. Underwear, I mean, so sorry, Ms. Underwood, what's the class policy on birthdays? Can we bring cupcakes or only low-sugar muffins?

Suddenly everyone was asking questions. And getting the teacher's name wrong.

Ms. Underwear!

Ms. Underwear!

Ms. Underwear!

Ms. Underwear!

Ms. Underwear!

Mr. Underwear!

Ms. Underwear!

Ms. Underwear!

Mr. Underwear!

Mr. Underwear!

Ms. Underwood didn't look happy. In fact, it looked like steam was coming out of her ears, she was so mad.

"I have been called Underwear since first grade! Please, please, PLEASE call me by my proper name, and I promise I'll do the same for all of you. No more name mess-ups."

Suddenly I was imagining Ms. Underwood as a little girl with big glasses and an unlucky name, just like my dad (except a girl).

I felt terrible.

At recess, I went up to her desk after everyone else had left.

"I'm sorry, Ms. Underwood. I shouldn't have gotten your name wrong," I said.

"That's okay," she said. "I shouldn't have gotten yours wrong, either. I'm usually much better than that."

Some kids still called me Daffy, but it wasn't horrible. Most got my name right. Though EVERYONE called Ms. Underwood Ms. Underwear — just not to her face. The fifth graders admitted they'd called her that all last year. I guess I shouldn't be surprised that I wasn't the first one to think up that nickname. She's been called that forever, I guess.

Today there were no after-school errands. I got to go straight home and have a snack with Donald and David.

The twins talked about sharing and reading <u>Frog and Toad</u>, and learning the Hokey Pokey. Now <u>that's</u> a funny name, I thought. Hokey Pokey!

It's especially funny if I think of the hamster doing it.

"And your day, Daphne?" Mom asked. "How was it? You know, you never told me if you like your teacher. Do you?"

"I can't tell yet," I said. "But so far she seems good. In fact, she reminds me of Dad in a way."

"Really? How?" Mom asked.

Dunston Dunce
↓

Underwear Underwood
↓

I could see them as little kids, the ones who always got teased by everyone else.

Of course, I wasn't going to say that to Mom.

So I shrugged. "I dunno. Just something."

And for once Mom didn't keep on asking. She got distracted by Donald and David and left me alone.

So I went to my room and started a list of all the names I'd be sure NOT to name my kids.

Daphne
Fiona
Bertha
Barbara
Mirka
Harriet

Dunston
Munster
Churchill
Winston
Lemuel
Dudley

Some of them sounded like burps (Bertha, Mirka) and some are just too terrible to impose on anyone. Like Harriet—there's no way to make that name anything but Harry It.

If my kid does end up being teased for their name, I hope they have a teacher like Ms. Underwood. Then _they_ can play the Name Game the way I did. And turn a disaster into a joke!

Bye now!

Looking at doodles
is okay, but NOT
looking at private
diaries!

doodles here
→

Absolutely NO
reading this diary!!
←

Disaster Doodles
↓

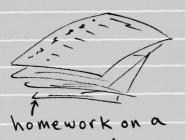

mud puddle

soggy, limp
french fries

homework on a
Friday!

dust
bunnies

tangled hair—ow!

Name Disasters

People who name everyone in the family with names starting with the same letter — way too cutesy-pie. Wait! That's my family!

Dad — Dunston Davis

Mom — Dolores Davis

David Davis

Donald Davis

and me, Daphne Davis

Maybe my name is a disaster even when it's pronounced the right way.

People who name their kids after days of the week or months. That can work for Tuesday, but NOT Wednesday and who wants to be Monday? For months, you can get away with May, June, April, even August (for a boy). But forget about November! And no February, either!

Nobody → looks like an October!

People who give their kids theme names — like all flowers.

Lily, Rose, Ivy

What a bouquet — too cute!

All colors.

Red — but not sunburned.

Gray — but not boring.

Blue — but not sad (just confused).

Red, Gray, and Blue. Almost patriotic, but not quite.

Or all places.

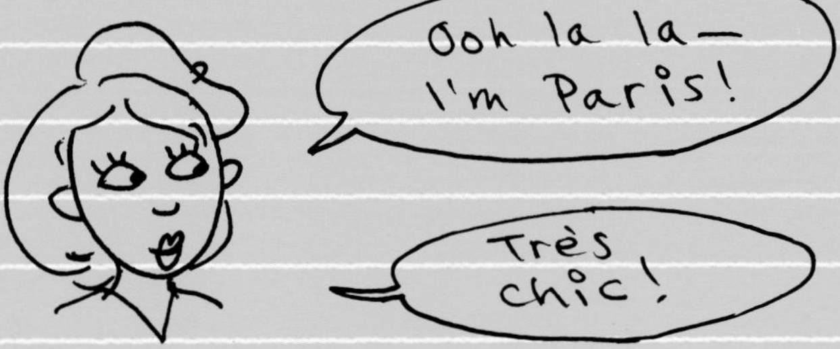

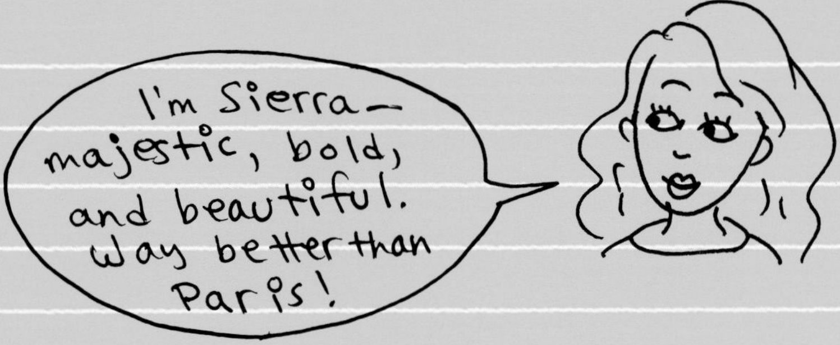

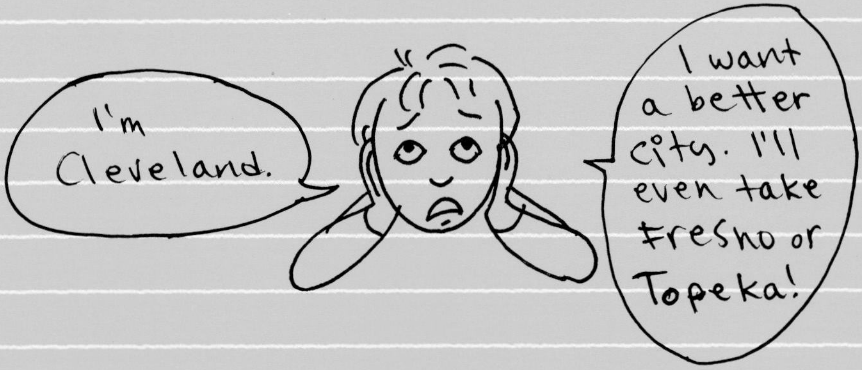

What's worse as a name—Modesto or Chattanooga?

People who give their kids dog names. Like Rex, Brutus, Duchess, Lady, Tramp. All are total disasters!

Worst of all, people who name their kids after condiments.

And there's Mustard, Ketchup, Relish, and the ever-popular Salsa. Not to mention Sauerkraut and Mayo. Plus all the spice names— Ginger, Cardamom, Paprika, and Cloves.

Kaylee, what are your name disasters?

Hmmm, I guess the time my uncle called me KayPee by accident. My cousins called me PeePee and WeeWee for the rest of the day.

Do they still do that?

They don't dare!

Oh, yeah? How come?

Because their names are Eli and Hester.

So?. Eli and Hester?.

So I called them
Eely and Pester. They
hated that! Now it's a
truce. Everyone gets called
by their right name.
Me and them.

So that trick
worked for you, but not
for me. How come?.

Dunno. Guess I had
better names to work
with.

Or you're more creative.

Well, what would you
call Eli and Hester?

Brown and Chester?
Some kind of dog name?
Condiment name? Color
name?. I GIVE UP!

Disaster Doodles

↓

boring assemblies

that panicky feeling that you forgot something important

Disaster Doodles
leaky pens
undercooked eggs with runny yolks-ICK!
Achoo!
sneezing without a tissue
Sorry about that! No snot is good snot.

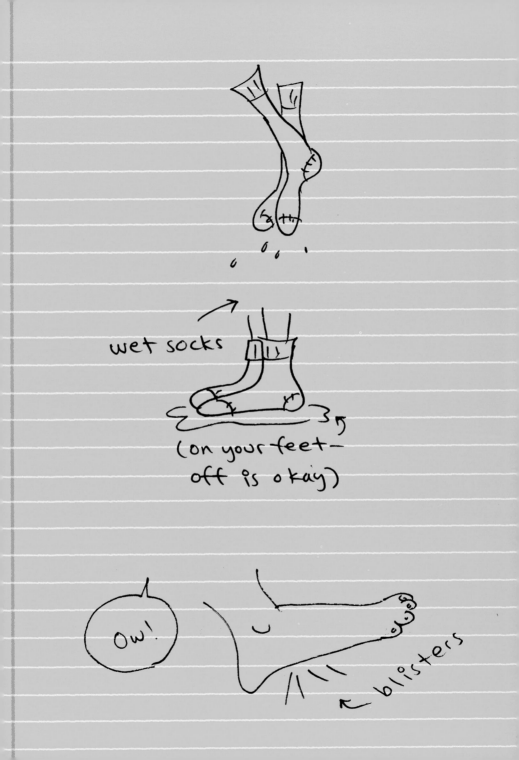

Unfavorite Disasters —
the Worst of the Worst!

Daily Disaster, Tuesday

1. Sardine sandwich in lunch.
2. Nobody will trade for stinky, fishy sandwich (can't blame them).
3. Eat sandwich (UGH!) or throw away and be hungry?
4. Throw away sandwich. (Was it ever really a choice?)
5. Lunch lady yells not to pollute the trash — sardine sandwich is worse than garbage!
6. Stomach growls until end of school when it's so loud, I can barely hear the bell ring.
7. Run home for snack and what's the only thing left in the refrigerator?
8. Sardines.

What's the worst disaster on the sole of your shoe?

dog poop?

gum?

squashed spider?

barf?

I DON'T WANT ANY OF THEM!

Cafeteria Menu

Advance warning of what NOT to eat!

Monday
Baked Chicken Tenders with Breadstick
Cheese Quesadilla
Peanut Butter & Jelly Sandwich

Tuesday
Hamburger on Wheat Bun
Spaghetti with Garlic Bread
Bagel & Cream Cheese

Wednesday
Grilled Cheese Sandwich
Turkey Hot Dog on Wheat Bun
Cheese Pizza

Thursday
Macaroni & Cheese
Beef & Bean Burrito
Turkey & Swiss Cheese Sandwich

Friday
Golden Trout Treasures
Chicken Teriyaki on Brown Rice
Turkey Corn Dog with Tater Tots

all this 3 wheat is supposed to make stuff somehow more nutritious — but not more delicious. Beware the smell alone!

Turkey somehow transforms a corn dog into a healthy food — kind of like ketchup counting as a vegetable. Either way, I call it a taste disaster!

Doughnut Doodles

↓

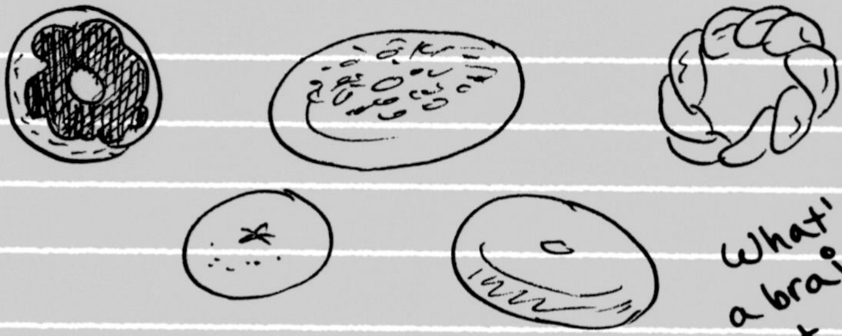

What's a braided doughnut called A broughnut

Donkey Doodles

↓

Delightful Doodles
↓

fresh-baked
chocolate chip
cookie—
mmmm!

happy baby—
how cute!

Disaster Doodles
↓

toast dropped
butter-side
down

angry, crying baby
with stinky diaper—
how horrible!